DORRIE
AND THE
MUSEUM CASE

story and pictures
by
Patricia Coombs

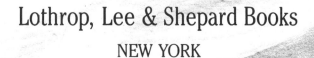

Lothrop, Lee & Shepard Books

NEW YORK

Library of Congress Cataloging in Publication Data

Coombs, Patricia.
    Dorrie and the museum case.

    Summary: With the help of her cousin Cosmo, Dorrie, the little witch, thwarts the scheme of Giblett the Enchanter on the opening day of the Witchville Museum.
    1. Children's stories, American.   [1. Witches—Fiction]   I. Title.
PZ7.C7813Dm 1986   [E]   84-27812
ISBN 0-688-04278-3
ISBN 0-688-04279-1 (lib. bdg.)

FOR MICHELE WEINER
and the Students of
Wrightstown Elementary School

This is Dorrie. She is a witch. A little witch. Her hat is always on crooked, and her socks never match. Sometimes her shoes are on the wrong feet. She lives with her mother, the Big Witch, and Cook, and her black cat, Gink.

One Friday morning, Dorrie's bed began to shake. The curtains twitched. Dorrie jumped out of bed, and so did Gink. Dorrie grabbed some socks and some shoes. She grabbed a dress. Her door flew open. The sheets flew off the bed. Her clothes whirled off the floor and the chair. Then they rolled up in a ball and whirled down the hall and down the stairs.

Dorrie got dressed. She looked at Gink and sighed. "I'll be glad when Cook gets back from her holiday," she said. She went into the hall and Gink went with her.

"How was it that time?" the Big Witch called out.

"A little better," said Dorrie. "I had time to get out of bed before the sheets took off."

Someone was knocking at the front door. Dorrie ran down the stairs and opened it. It was the Post-Witch. "Special Delivery," she said. "It's from your Uncle Flagstone."

Dorrie took the letter up, up, up the stairs to the Big Witch's secret room. The cauldron was bubbling and steaming and smelled like soap.

"A letter came, Mother. It's from Uncle Flagstone."

Dorrie stirred while the Big Witch read the letter. The Big Witch groaned.

"Your Uncle Flagstone is going to fly around the world," she said. "He is dropping off Cousin Cosmo in Witches' Meadow, *today*!" The Big Witch looked at the clock. "He'll be there any minute!"

"Oh, good!" said Dorrie.

"Oh, bad!" said the Big Witch. "Today is the grand opening of the Oddson-Ends Museum. I'm giving a speech, I'm in charge of the tea and the tour, and I haven't finished the house-cleaning spells! And now Cosmo is coming to visit!"

"Don't worry," said Dorrie. "I'll keep Cosmo so busy you won't even know we're around."

A few minutes later, Dorrie and Gink and the Big Witch landed in Witches' Meadow.

"He must be here," said Dorrie, looking all around. "I see his suitcase beside that big rock."

"But where is *he*?" snapped the Big Witch. "I have to be at the museum in fifteen minutes to get everything set up. I have a hundred things to do!"

"Never mind," said Dorrie. "I'll find Cousin Cosmo. You just take his suitcase with you, and we'll walk home."

"That's a good idea. Thank you." The Big Witch picked up the bag, got on her broomstick, and flew away.

Dorrie and Gink climbed on top of the big rock. Dorrie looked across the meadow. She saw something in a tree. "Come on, Gink. I think we just found Cosmo."

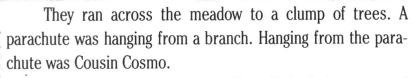

They ran across the meadow to a clump of trees. A parachute was hanging from a branch. Hanging from the parachute was Cousin Cosmo.

"Hi, Cosmo," said Dorrie. She climbed the tree and unhooked the parachute. Cosmo slid to the ground.

"Thanks, Dorrie," he said. "Have you seen my suitcase? I was coming down too fast, and so I dropped it."

"Mother has it. She had to leave in a hurry. Cook is on a holiday, and so Mother is using spells to clean house. And today is the grand opening of the Oddson-Ends Museum.

"A museum?" asked Cosmo. "It sounds dull."

"Not this one," said Dorrie. "Witch Oddson and Witch Ends gave the house to the town. It's dark and spooky, and Witch Ends says the place is haunted. Everybody gave a lot of old magic things so you can see the whole history of Witchville. Come on," she said, leading the way across the meadow. "Mother must be home by now, and I'm hungry."

Not far away, in the only house left in Eel Flats, Giblett the Enchanter sniffed the mixture in his cauldron and smiled a mean smile. He peered into the old book beside him. His smile faded. *"In the last hour of the last Friday of the tenth month, stir the potion in an old bowl of Chinese brass. The power of the potion comes from the bowl."*

Giblett began to pace back and forth. "Today is the last Friday of the tenth month! I only have until midnight to find such a bowl, or all my work is lost!" he cried. "Somewhere, somewhere I once saw a bowl like that. Think, Giblett! Use your bean!"

He stopped. "That's it! Beans! A bowl full of jellybeans! At Witch Ends's house the night they banished me from Witchville!"

With his cloak flapping, his hat pulled down, and his collar pulled up, Giblett flew off to Witch Ends's house. When he knocked, Witch Ends answered through the door.

"Go away!" she shouted. "I'm washing my hair. Come back tomorrow."

"Tomorrow will be too late!" cried Giblett. "I will give you a bag of gold for your old Chinese brass bowl."

"I don't want any gold," said Witch Ends crossly. "I want to wash my hair. Besides, I gave that old bowl to our museum. Today is the grand opening, and I must get ready."

Hiding in the clouds, Giblett flew slowly over Witchville. "Heh-heh," he chuckled to himself. "Fools! To think they could banish *me*."

Dorrie, Cosmo, and Gink were walking across Dorrie's front yard when the door blew open. Rugs and carpets came flying out and knocked them over. Then they rolled up with Dorrie and Cosmo and Gink inside, sailed back into the house, and unrolled. Dorrie and Cosmo and Gink sat up. Gink sneezed. Doors and windows were opening and closing. A pile of laundry whirled past them.

"How was it that time?" called the Big Witch.

"The rugs are all right, except that they still use the front door. And the laundry still stops at the top of the cellar stairs," said Dorrie. "Your spells are getting a lot better."

"This is better?" said Cosmo. "I'm glad I wasn't here last week."

The Big Witch leaned over the banister. "There's some soup for you and Cosmo simmering on the stove. I'm going to take a nap now. Housework is *very* tiring, and I must be at my best tonight."

"May we go to the museum after lunch?" asked Dorrie. "We'd like to look around before the crowd gets there."

"All right," said the Big Witch. "But stay out of trouble, and *don't* touch the exhibits."

Dorrie and Cosmo went into the kitchen. They made peanut butter sandwiches. Cosmo poured the milk while Dorrie filled their soup bowls. She gave a bowl to Gink, too.

"Wow!" said Cosmo. "This is good soup."

"It sure is," said Dorrie. "Funny, though, I thought Mother was going to make chicken-noodle soup. I don't see any noodles in this."

"Maybe the noodles are in the laundry," said Cosmo.

After lunch they walked down the path, through the woods, and along the road that led to Witchville. Soon they saw the pointy roofs of the town poking up above the trees.

Witchville was very quiet. Everybody was taking a nap or shining their best shoes or ironing their best hats. Nobody saw Giblett land behind the museum. Nobody saw him sneak inside, carrying a suitcase.

Flags were flying from the towers when Dorrie and Cosmo and Gink got to the door of the museum. A sign in front creaked in the wind. Dorrie turned to Cosmo. "Quit bumping into me...Cosmo! What are you doing? You're fading! Stop that!"

ODDSON-ENDS MUSEUM
of
HISTORY, MYSTERY
and
MAGIC ARTS

"I can't stop it!" said Cosmo. "You're fading, too! And look at Gink. He looks like a ghost cat!"

"Oh-oh," said Dorrie. "I think we're in trouble."

"You're wrong," said Cosmo. "We can't be in trouble if no one can see us. Wow! This is great!"

Dorrie looked at Cosmo. She looked at Gink. "Well," she said, "we just won't bother to tell Mother until *after* the grand opening."

They went inside. The hall was big and dark, with doors and stairs all around. There were statues and paintings and vases and stuffed bats and broomsticks.

They wandered all about, looking at the exhibits. "Hey, Dorrie," called Cosmo. "This looks like my suitcase. Over here, behind this statue."

Dorrie went over and looked. "Oh, I know what happened. Mother's been so busy, she must have left it behind this morning. We'll take it with us when we go. Come on, let's explore."

Up, up, up the stairs they went, and Gink went with them. Down, down, down the long, dark halls they went, in and out of all the rooms. They looked at old books and bones and fossils and stones and cabinets full of magic things. There were old dishes and shoes and quilts and tools and pots and pans.

They came at last to some narrow, crooked stairs. "What's up there?" asked Cosmo.

"The topmost tower. It's the spookiest of all,"said Dorrie. "It's my favorite place. Come on."

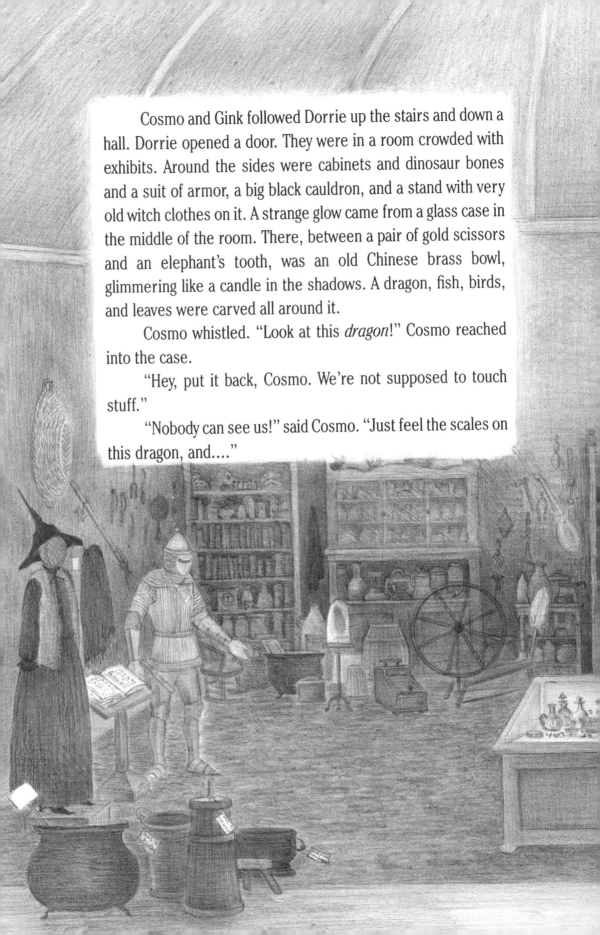

Cosmo and Gink followed Dorrie up the stairs and down a hall. Dorrie opened a door. They were in a room crowded with exhibits. Around the sides were cabinets and dinosaur bones and a suit of armor, a big black cauldron, and a stand with very old witch clothes on it. A strange glow came from a glass case in the middle of the room. There, between a pair of gold scissors and an elephant's tooth, was an old Chinese brass bowl, glimmering like a candle in the shadows. A dragon, fish, birds, and leaves were carved all around it.

Cosmo whistled. "Look at this *dragon*!" Cosmo reached into the case.

"Hey, put it back, Cosmo. We're not supposed to touch stuff."

"Nobody can see us!" said Cosmo. "Just feel the scales on this dragon, and...."

They heard something. There were footsteps in the hall. Someone else was in the tower! The footsteps grew louder and louder, closer and closer. They stopped.

Dorrie and Cosmo and Gink backed into the darkest part of the room. "Hide the bowl," whispered Dorrie. "Whoever it is can't see us, but they can see the bowl shining."

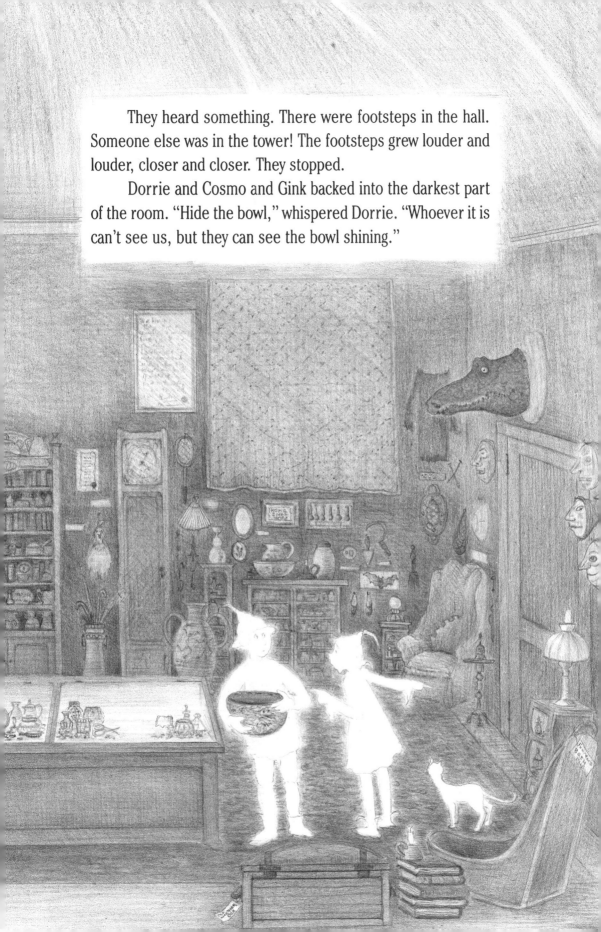

Slowly the door creaked open. A dark figure stepped in and scurried over to the case. "The bowl, the bowl. It isn't downstairs so it must be *here*!" he muttered. Around and around he went, like a big black crab, peering everywhere. He came so close to Dorrie and Cosmo his whiskers brushed their faces. Suddenly he snapped his fingers, dashed out the door, and disappeared.

"Who was that creepy person?" asked Cosmo.

"Giblett the Enchanter! He's dyed his hair and grown a beard, but it's Giblett. He makes up such nasty spells, he's been banished. He hates Witchville. He wouldn't dare come back here unless...unless he'd discovered some magic more powerful than Mother's!"

"He's looking for something," said Cosmo. "I heard him muttering about a bowl. It must be *this* bowl! We've got to keep it away from him."

"And we've got to find out why he wants it. We'll just have to follow him. But first, let's put on some of these old clothes so we can see each other." Dorrie took the hat off the stand and put it on. She took the vest and gave it to Cosmo. She tied a ribbon around Gink's neck.

"That's a lot better," said Cosmo. "Now we've got to hide the bowl. It's too heavy to carry around, and he might see it shining."

"I know, the tea party!" said Dorrie. "Giblett said he'd looked downstairs. That means he's been in the parlor. Once Mother and the other witches and wizards are there, I don't think he'd risk being seen."

Down the stairs they crept. At every door and every corner, they listened. There were no sounds of Giblett. At last they reached the front hall.

Cosmo stood watch while Dorrie carried the Chinese bowl into the parlor. She put it in the middle of the table and filled it with candy corn. Then she placed the plates of cakes and cookies and sandwiches all around it, and hurried back into the hall.

"Hey, Dorrie, over here," whispered Cosmo. "Look! Another suitcase, just like mine."

"Giblett's!" they both whispered at once.

"It has to be his," said Dorrie. "No one else has been in the museum. I bet he's got some awful spell inside it."

Cosmo nodded. "He's got it locked with a spell, too. I can't open it. We've got to hide it so he can't use it."

"Put your suitcase where Giblett's was," said Dorrie.

Just then they heard all the witches and wizards landing in front of the museum.

"Quick, this way," whispered Dorrie, hurrying toward a doorway under the stairs. She opened another door. "Here, Cosmo. This is the broom closet. Hide the suitcase behind those buckets and mops."

Down the hall was another door. They stopped and listened. "This goes to the cellar," whispered Dorrie. "I bet he's down there."

They opened the door quietly, tiptoed partway down the stairs, and looked. A single candle was flickering. There was Giblett, rummaging in a big box. Empty boxes and barrels were piled all around him. He was scowling and muttering. All at once he stood up. He had something in his hands.

"Oh-oh," whispered Cosmo. "A crystal ball!"
Then the words of Giblett's chant drifted around them:

"O sphere of glass, alas,
A Chinese bowl someone hath taken;
Show me, show, O crystal ball,
Who swiped that magic bowl of brass.
Show me their image in thy glass,
That I may catch and snatch it from them!"

Dorrie and Cosmo and Gink watched Giblett rub his sleeve over the ball and peer into it. He rubbed it again. And again. "Bah!" he snarled. "This ball is no good. They look like *ghosts*. Two short ghosts. I can see a vest very clearly. And a hat. Whoever they are, I'll soon turn them into puffs of smoke."

Dorrie and Cosmo and Gink got to the top of the stairs just before Giblett. They stood very still beside a hat rack. Giblett brushed past them and peered into the front hall. He saw the Big Witch. All the witches and wizards were crowded around her. The grand tour was starting.

Giblett hissed through his teeth, "Somewhere in that crowd are the two I have to catch. But I mustn't be seen. Ah-ha!" He snapped his fingers. As soon as the witches and wizards went into a room, Giblett scurried up the stairs to the tower. Dorrie and Cosmo and Gink raced after him.

Five minutes later, Giblett hurried down from the tower to find the tour. A black shawl was tied over his head, and he was wearing a blouse and a long black skirt. He heard the Big Witch saying, "Now we'll look in this room. On the wall is the first Witchville flag. And this is the loom...."

Giblett lurked in the shadows at the back of the room, searching for a vest and a hat in the crowd. Dorrie and Cosmo and Gink stayed close behind him. In one room and out the other they went. Room by room by room, Giblett followed the witches and wizards, and Dorrie and Cosmo followed Giblett. Everyone was crowded so closely around the Big Witch, Giblett couldn't see any short witches or wizards. Time was running out. Giblett glared at his watch and bit his nails.

An hour later, the Big Witch led her group up the narrow crooked stairs and down the hall to the tower room. "In here, we have some of our oldest treasures," she said. "In this glass case you'll see a pair of gold scissors and...umm, a lucky elephant's tooth. Over here is the cauldron used by the founder of Witchville. The first spell in Witchville was mixed in that cauldron with this spoon. And here we have her favorite clothes."

When the Big Witch pointed to the stand, the crowd began to giggle. All that was left on it was some long black underwear and two pointy boots.

"Hmm," murmured the Big Witch. "Our Chinese brass bowl and the founder's clothes?"

"I told you the place is haunted. That's why we gave it away," said Witch Ends.

"Do hush," said Witch Oddson. "The clothes must be at the cleaners."

The Big Witch clapped her hands. "Time for tea!" she said, leading everyone back down the hall and down the stairs and back to the parlor. Giblett sidled out from behind a vase and crept after them.

"Oh, where are those two bowl-snatchers!" he hissed, clenching his fists. "If it weren't for them, I'd have been safely home with the bowl hours ago."

The crowd moved into the parlor. While the Big Witch poured the tea, all the witches and wizards chatted and filled their plates. Giblett watched them from the doorway. Then he edged into the room, crouching behind a vase of ferns. Dorrie and Cosmo and Gink hid behind the drapes.

"I didn't think he'd risk coming in here," whispered Dorrie. "I've got to get the bowl and hide it again."

Just then, they heard Giblett gasp.

"We're too late! He sees the bowl!" whispered Cosmo. "He saw it when Witch Ends moved that plate of cakes."

"I've got to get it!" whispered Dorrie. "You keep him away, Cosmo!"

Dorrie made her way among the witches and wizards. They were too busy talking and eating to notice the hat. She took the brass bowl of candy corn and began to pass it around. Giblett, the shawl tied over his head, followed the bowl with glittering eyes. Cosmo followed Giblett. Around and around and around, through the crowd they went, faster and faster.

One by one, the witches and wizards stopped talking. They stopped eating. They began to back up until they were all huddled together at one end of the room.

The Chinese bowl was flying through the air in front of an old black hat. A bearded witch with glasses on was trying to grab the bowl. A vest with no one in it was chasing the witch with the beard.

"I told you the place was haunted," said Witch Ends.

"This is one of the Big Witch's surprises," said Witch Oddson. "A pageant. That's the ghost of the founder of Witchville."

"I don't remember the founder of Witchville having a beard," said Witch Ends.

All at once, Giblett picked up a chair and threw it, knocking Dorrie down. The bowl sailed out of her hands and into the hall. Giblett was after it in a flash. Cosmo made a flying tackle, and

down went Giblett, kicking and yelling. He swung his fists and hit Cosmo in the head. Cosmo tumbled backward, letting go of Giblett's ankles.

Giblett the Enchanter leaped into the hall and grabbed the suitcase. "I've got you now!" he yelled.

"Abracadabra, nitter natter,
Make these witches, wizards dizzy!
Turn their spells to howls and chatter!"

With that, Giblett whirled the suitcase around and around, scattering everything in it over the crowd of witches and wizards.

It was the wrong suitcase. Instead of a magic spell, Cosmo's socks and his pajamas, his underwear, his galoshes, two shirts, his green slippers, and his blue toothbrush flew through the air.

Clutching the bowl, Giblett ran to the front door. The bowl was growing brighter and brighter. Giblett began tossing it from one hand to the other. It was growing hotter and hotter and *hotter.* Giblett screeched and dropped the glowing bowl.

Meanwhile, the Big Witch was spinning and chanting. She pointed her finger at Giblett. He was whirled out the door and into the darkness, still screeching.

"Wow!" said Cosmo. "That spell works a lot better on a wicked Enchanter than it does on the laundry."

Dorrie went over and picked up the bowl. "It isn't hot anymore," she said.

"See? I told you so," said Witch Ends. "Even the bowl is haunted. It speaks and is followed by a hat."

"It speaks with a voice I know," said the Big Witch. "Dorrie, are you there?"

"Yes, Mother," said Dorrie.

"Me, too," said Cosmo. "My head hurts."

"We can explain," said Dorrie. "We didn't mean to be invisible, but we...."

"I know," said the Big Witch. "I went to the stove to get the spot and stain remover, and it was almost all gone. You'd each had two helpings, and the soup kettle was still full."

"That explains it," said Dorrie.

"Explains what?" said Cosmo.

"Why there weren't any noodles in it," said Dorrie.

Everyone went back into the parlor to finish their tea and talk about their narrow escape from Giblett's spells. Witch Ends picked up the brass bowl. "I seem to remember our great-grandmother telling us something about this bowl," she murmured. "*Its powers cannot be used for ill.* That was it!"

Dorrie and Cosmo took Giblett's suitcase from the broom closet and gave it to the Big Witch.

"We think this suitcase contains the magic spell Giblett was going to use on us while he escaped with the bowl," said Dorrie.

"I think we'll drop it off in Black Pond on our way home," said the Big Witch.

And that's just what they did. Then the Big Witch led Dorrie and Cosmo and Gink up into her secret room. She mixed up some magic crystals and dust and sprinkled it over them. They watched themselves grow visible again.

"Wow!" said Cosmo.

They all went down to the kitchen and had great big bowls of real chicken-noodle soup.

"Now I'll try my new dishwashing spell," said the Big Witch.

"Oh, no!" Dorrie and Cosmo said together. "*We'll* do the dishes by ourselves."

And they did.